THE
BOOSEY BRASS
METHOD

series editor:

CHRIS MORGAN

Eb **brass band instruments** 𝄞 **book 1**

BOOSEY & HAWKES

London · New York · Berlin · Sydney

Series editor: Chris Morgan

Chris Morgan began teaching in 1974 and has been committed to instrumental teacher and curriculum development since 1979, when he was appointed Head of Woodwind for the Inner London Education Authority (ILEA). Subsequent posts have included Head of Instrumental Services with ILEA, Director of Instrumental Teacher Training at Guildhall School of Music & Drama, London, responsibility for professional and curriculum development with Cornwall Education Authority, and as a provider of professional development programmes with the Associated Board of the Royal Schools of Music, Guildhall School of Music & Drama and numerous music services in the UK and elsewhere. He is currently co-director of Music and Dance Education, based in Cornwall.

Brass specialist: Ian Lowes, Head of Composition, Bryanston School and CT ABRSM brass mentor

Editorial board:

Jo Coventry, Northamptonshire Music and Performing Arts Service

Cathy Elliott, Junior School, Guildhall School of Music & Drama, London

Andreas Gafke, W. Schreiber & Söhne GmbH (Keilwerth Saxophones)

Eric Hollis, Director of Initial Studies, Guildhall School of Music & Drama, London

Stephen Richards, Director of Educational Publishing, Boosey & Hawkes Music Publishers Ltd.

Peter Wastall, woodwind and brass consultant, Boosey & Hawkes Music Publishers Ltd.

Boosey & Hawkes acknowledges the assistance of the Guildhall School of Music & Drama in developing the curriculum framework used in this series.

Feeling the Rhythm activities by Pat Hickman, co-director of Music and Dance Education
Music setting by Artemis Music Ltd.
Illustrations by Valerie Hill
Recordings by CN Productions
Cover design by Electric Echo
Printed by Halstan & Co. Ltd., Amersham, Bucks., England

INTRODUCTION

The Boosey Woodwind and Brass Method is designed to be used in lessons and when you play your instrument between lessons. To get the most out of the book, work through it with your teacher, playing the music and doing the activities. The CDs will help you between lessons - it contains performances and backing tracks of most of the pieces in the book, as well as listening activities.

At the end of the book you will find checklists for each stage. These help you to keep track of what you have learned. When you reach the end of a stage, fill in the checklist with your teacher. If there are gaps, try to finish the activities before you go on to the next stage. The activities are designed to help you explore music and improve as a musician.

Remember, different people learn at different speeds. Try not to rush. Work at a pace that feels comfortable. That way you will learn faster, and enjoy playing more.

This book is divided into nine sections - a "basics" section and eight stages. The basics pages (4-7) are orange and contain information about your instrument (how to hold it, how to look after it) and exercises to help you get started. Keep referring back to this section to remind yourself how to do these correctly.

Stages 1 to 8 teach you how to play your instrument and how to make music come alive. In addition to pieces to play, there are many different types of activities for you to do. The icons below have been designed to help you. Each one has a different meaning.

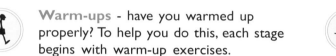 **Warm-ups** - have you warmed up properly? To help you do this, each stage begins with warm-up exercises.

Breathing activity - are you breathing in the right way? See page 6 for more about this.

Feel the rhythm - this could mean clapping, moving, counting, singing or two of these things at once.

Clap or sing - there are some tunes and activities for clapping or singing, and others which you clap or sing first, then play.

Write or record - sometimes you will find activities which include writing things down or making a recording.

Sometimes you will find hints and extra activities in the margins

Ensemble - this icon means you can play the piece with anyone learning from any *Boosey Brass* or *Boosey Woodwind* book.

 Use the CDs - select the track number in the icon. You may have to listen - or you may be asked to sing or play along.

It will help if you keep a notebook and use it specially for your lessons and projects

Answer a question - or solve a puzzle, or think about something in a different way.

Using the CD

Books in the *Boosey Woodwind and Brass Method* include two CDs:

*   **performance CD** - use this CD to hear complete performances of the music
*   **backing CD** - use this CD to play along with

Both CDs contain the same music so the track listings are identical. Each recording begins with clicks to show you at what speed to play.

You will also find tuning notes on the CD - **G** on track 2 and **C** on track 22.

Additional web resources, including backing tracks, extra pieces and activities are available for *The Boosey Woodwind and Brass Method*. Visit **www.boosey.com** for further information.

For extra repertoire for use with stages 1-4, see *Boosey Brass E♭ Brass Band Instruments Repertoire book A*. For extra repertoire for use with stages 5-8, see *Boosey Brass E♭ Brass Band Instruments Repertoire book B*.

you will find a summary at the bottom of each page in this book

Parts of a tenor horn and E♭ bass

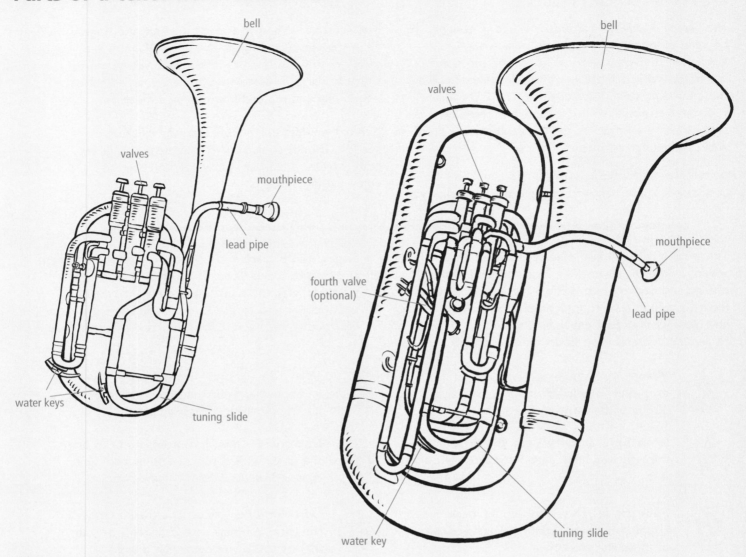

bell

valves

bell

valves

mouthpiece

lead pipe

mouthpiece

fourth valve
(optional)

lead pipe

water keys

tuning slide

water key

tuning slide

Holding your instrument

Ask your teacher for more help with this. Lay
your instrument case somewhere safe before
opening the lid - on a table or on the floor. Make
sure that your hands are clean, as dirt can damage
your instrument. Be careful not to drop or bang
your instrument - brass is soft and dents easily.

Lift your instrument out of the case and
place it on your lap with the bell
pointing up and with the lead pipe
pointing towards you. Put your left
arm around the front of the
instrument to support its weight,
which with the tenor horn will lift
the instrument off your lap. If your
E♭ bass has a fourth valve, your left-
hand index finger should be placed
to operate this. Take the mouthpiece
and place it into the instrument. The
mouthpiece should be gently twisted,
never banged into place.

Arch your right hand as if you were holding an orange in the palm. Rest your thumb against the tubing next to the valves and place your little finger on the tube or inside the finger hook if there is one. The pads of your remaining fingers should rest on the valve caps. Always keep your hand in this position ("don't squash your orange!") and keep your wrist straight. Remember to push the valves straight down into their casings.

How to stand or sit when playing

You should stand or sit upright, but keep your body balanced and relaxed. Place both feet flat on the floor, slightly apart. Always bring the instrument to your lips - never take your lips to the mouthpiece.

If you are sitting, use a chair without arms and sit on the front half of the chair. If you are using a music stand, make sure it is at the right height for you. The angle of the instrument should remain the same if you are standing or sitting and your arms should be relaxed and not held tightly into your body.

Depending on your size and the size of the instrument, you may wish to rest the instrument in your lap. If you do this, make sure that you are still bringing the instrument to your lips. If you feel tired and can't hold your instrument up, stop and have a rest.

Breathing

When you play your instrument, you will need to breathe differently from usual. At first it is a good idea to practise breathing without holding your instrument.

Breathing in (inhaling)

Open your throat, as if you are yawning. Take a deep breath in through your mouth. When you breathe in, your shoulders should stay still. Your stomach and your whole ribcage will spread outwards. (If you push your hands gently on your stomach as you breathe in, you will feel this).

Breathing out (exhaling)

Breathe out slowly from your lower stomach. Keep the flow of air steady - imagine you are blowing up a balloon or blowing bubbles. When you breathe out, your cheeks should not puff out. Your stomach and ribcage will move inwards again as you breathe out.

Forming an embouchure and making a sound

An embouchure (say "om - boo - sure") is the position of your lips, teeth, tongue and cheeks that you use when playing. Everybody's embouchure is different. Ask your teacher for more help.

With your teeth in line (or as near in line as is comfortable) but slightly apart, firm your lips against your front teeth. Imagine you are holding a straw in your lips. Take a deep breath and blow out through the imaginary straw, without making a sound. Be careful not to puff out your cheeks.

Try to ensure that the air comes straight out, as if blowing through the an imaginary straw. Try this again but grip the straw harder so that your lips vibrate to produce a **buzzing** sound. This is the basis of producing a sound on your instrument.

Mouthpiece buzzing

Take your mouthpiece on its own and hold it with your thumb and forefinger. Moisten your lips then place the lower rim just below your bottom lip. There should be slightly more top lip in the mouthpiece for the tenor horn but roughly twice as much for the E♭ bass. Buzz into the mouthpiece in exactly the same way as you did without it.

Breathe in as before but through the corners of your mouth so that the mouthpiece stays on your lips. Keep a steady buzz and avoid puffing your cheeks out. Keep the mouthpiece pressure to a minimum (your lips are a cushion for the mouthpiece to rest on).

 You can hear what a mouthpiece buzz sounds like on track 97 of the CD.

To make a clean start to each buzz, use your tongue as if saying the word "**dah**". The tip of your tongue should be touching the bottom edge of your top teeth when you start to make each sound (but should not come between your teeth).

Practise this tongued buzz several times:

| buzz | rest | buzz |
| buzz | rest | buzz |

Replace the mouthpiece in the instrument, bring it to your lips, take a deep breath and breathe out through the instrument, making the buzz at the same time. You should have your first note.

Practise holding steady notes for as long as you can. Also play long notes broken up into shorter sounds by using your tongue to "dah" the start of each note. Your tongue should only be used to start notes, not to stop them.

 You have probably discovered it is possible to play a few different types of buzzing sounds and notes. Practise the note that you can play when your embouchure is relaxed, as heard on track 2. Is the note you play like that on the CD? If it is very different you may need to alter your embouchure. Ask your teacher for help with this.

Buzzing exercises should form part of your "warm up" routine each time you play. To help you do this, each stage of *The Boosey Brass Method E♭ Brass Band Instruments* book 1 begins with a *Warm-ups* section. Every time you use this book, be sure to practise the *Warm-ups* of the stage that you are working on.

Looking after your instrument

It is important to store your instrument safely in its case as it may easily dent and this will affect the playing quality. Always transport it in its case. Secure your mouthpiece and other accessories as they can come loose and damage your instrument. Never put anything in the case that will make it difficult to close the lid, for example, lots of sheet music.

When you have finished playing, twist the mouthpiece free and replace it in the case. Open the water key to drain excess moisture and return the tuning slide to the closed position. Use a soft, clean cloth (a special polishing cloth is best) to remove dust and fingerprints from your instrument. Place the instrument firmly in the case and make sure the case is properly closed before lifting it up.

Caring for valves

The valves are an extremely important part of your instrument. In order to look after them, they will need to be oiled regularly. Ask your teacher for more help with this. Unscrew the valve at the top of the valve casing and gently pull out the valve, remembering how it is aligned. Wipe clean with a lint-free cloth. Coat the entire valve sparingly with special **valve oil**, available from most music shops. Carefully return the valve to its casing, ensuring it is aligned correctly. The top of the valve should now easily screw back into place.

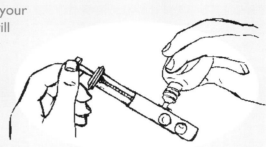

Caring for the tuning slide

The tuning slide is also an important part of your instrument and needs to be cleaned regularly. Remove the slide and clean it with a tissue or a lint-free cloth. Then apply a thin layer of petroleum jelly or specialist slide grease. Replace the slide and move in and out to ensure the tuning slide grease is evenly spread. Remove any excess with a cloth.

Tuning

You may find that your instrument sounds slightly higher or lower than the same note on the CD or other instruments. If it does you will need to adjust it - this is called tuning. You do this by moving the tuning slide - ask your teacher for help with this.

Tune your instrument to the note **G** (see page 8). Play track 2 of the CD to hear this note then play **G** on your instrument. Listen carefully to both notes. Is your note the same, or is it slightly higher or lower than the CD?

If your note is higher than the tuning note, you will need to pull out the main tuning slide by a tiny amount. If it is lower, gently push the main tuning slide in.

There is no set position for the main tuning slide, and you will find that its position will vary each time you play.

Golden Rules

• Never let your lips or cheeks puff out

• Keep the mouthpiece in the middle of your mouth

• Always touch the mouthpiece lightly against your lips and don't press - it should never leave a dent on your lips

• Always tongue against your teeth, don't let your tongue come between your teeth

• Breathe deeply before playing, don't move your shoulders as you breathe in

• Always strive for a good quality sound, don't blow too loudly

• Always moisten your lips before playing

Warm-ups

See the mouthpiece buzzing exercise on page 6

Always use these exercises to warm up before playing any part of stage 1

Using only the mouthpiece, buzz these blocks. Don't forget to use your tongue to start each block.

| long | rest | | long | rest |

Now buzz shorter sounds.

| shor- | ter | rest | | shor- | ter | rest |

Then buzz these patterns of long and shorter sounds.

| long | rest | | shor- | ter | rest |
| shor- | ter | rest | | long | rest |

Echo Games

Make up your own Echo Games too

With your teacher, buzz or clap these *Echo Games*:

 echo   echo

echo   echo

Playing G

Notes which do not use any valves are called "open" notes

To play the note **G** you do not need to use any of the valves, but keep your fingers resting on the valve caps. You can hear **G** on track 2 of the CD, or ask your teacher to play it.
    This is what **G** looks like written down:

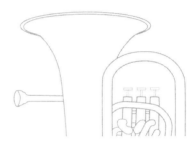

0

Starting Blocks

Use **G** to play these blocks - slowly at first, then a little faster:

| long | rest | | shor- | ter | rest |
| shor- | ter | rest | | long | rest |

Fanfare Time

Create your own pattern of long and shorter notes to go with Fanfare Time

Join in with *Fanfare Time* on track 1 of the CD. Here is your part written as blocks. Wait for the opening fanfare to finish, then play your part four times on the note **G**. Take a breath after each long note.

This is what your part for *Fanfare Time* looks like written out as music.

Music is written on sets of five lines called a *staff*.

This sign is called a *treble clef*. You will see this at the beginning of each line of music.

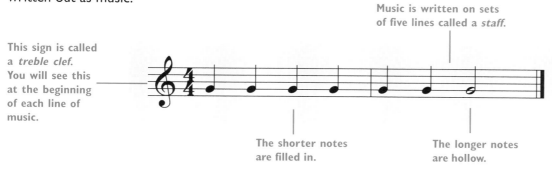

The shorter notes are filled in.

The longer notes are hollow.

One Two Watch

The sound on track 3 is called a **pulse**. A pulse keeps going without changing. It's like the ticking of a watch or clock. Each sound of the pulse is called a **beat**. A pattern of notes of different lengths is called a **rhythm**.

stem —

note-head

A one-beat note is called a *crotchet* or *quarter note*. It has a filled-in notehead.

A two-beat note is called a *minim* or *half note*. It has a hollow notehead.

There is a pulse in most of the music you have ever listened to, danced to, sung or played

First, play the rhythm written as blocks.

Now play the rhythm again, using the note symbols.

This sign tells you to take a breath.

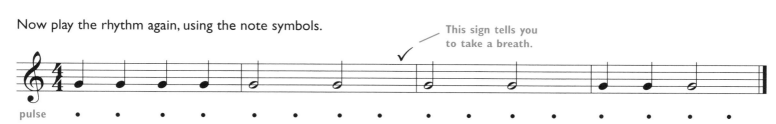

Feeling the Rhythm

You can speak in rhythm, clap, tap your feet, dance - even think in rhythm. Say the words below and clap or step the rhythms with the pulse on track 3 of the CD.

Can you think up some other words to fit with either of the rhythms?

Rhythm Grid

Look at the rhythms in the grid. You can work across, up or down the grid in any order you like. Using the backing on track **4** as an accompaniment, try the following:

- Buzz or clap the rhythms.
- Sing the rhythms on any note you like.
- "Think" the rhythms in your head.
- Play the rhythms using **G**.

Echo Games

With your teacher, buzz, clap, sing or play these *Echo Games*:

E-zy to Play

Clap or buzz the rhythm of this tune. Have you clapped it or played it before? Then play it using the note **G**.

This sign is called a *time signature*. The 4 at the top tells you that the beats come in groups of four - there are four beats in each bar.

Usually you feel beats in groups. These groups are called *bars* or *measure*s.

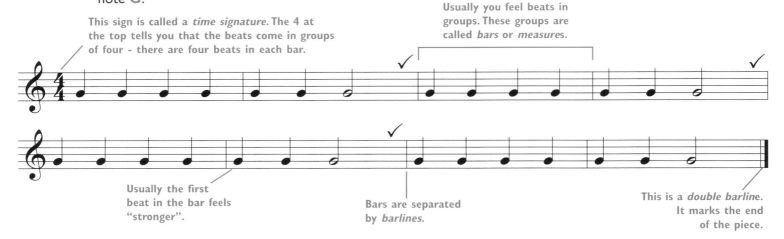

Usually the first beat in the bar feels "stronger".

Bars are separated by *barlines*.

This is a *double barline*. It marks the end of the piece.

Listen to some of your favourite music and decide how the beats are grouped - in twos, threes, fours?

High Hopes

Remember to take a breath where you see the sign.

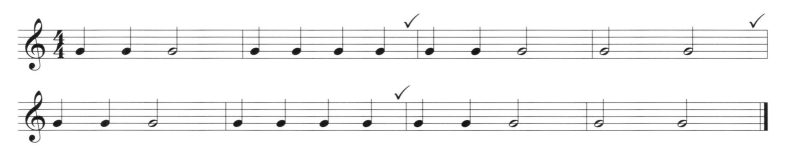

Feeling the Rhythm

Count or step the pulse and clap the rhythm.
Turn your palms upwards for each rest.

This sign is a two-beat rest. It tells you not to play for two beats.

Clap:

Step or say: 1   2   3   4   1   2   3   4   1   2   3   4   1   2   3   4

On the Spot

Listen to track 7 on the CD and count with the pulse which you can hear in the low notes of the piano part.

Then play *On the Spot* using the note **G**. During the rests, count the beat carefully and take a breath.

This sign is a whole-bar rest. It tells you not to play for a whole bar.

Count   1   2   3   4   1   2   3   4

In and Out

You don't need to use your instrument for *In and Out*. You can do this anywhere - going to school, in the bath, watching TV.

Breathe in				Breathe out			
count				*count*			
1	**2**	**3**	**4**	**1**	**2**	**3**	**4**

Go! Stop!

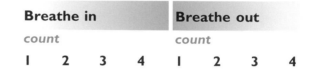

1   2   3   4

You can play *Go! Stop!* using other rhythms too.

Instead of  try one of the rhythms on the right:    or

High and low

Sing a high note followed by a low note, then a low note followed by a high note. **Pitch** is the word for how high or low a note is.

Using your mouthpiece only, buzz a higher sound and a lower sound. In order to play a higher buzz, tighten or 'firm' your embouchure very slightly to make your lips vibrate faster. You will also need to provide faster air support. Ask your teacher for help.

Higher

breathe   breathe   breathe

Lower

Playing F

Have you warmed up properly? Go to page 8

To play the note **F** press down the first valve. Make sure you press the valve straight down and that it goes all the way down. **F** is lower in pitch than **G**, therefore you will also need to relax your embouchure slightly and provide slower air.

This is what **F** looks like written down:

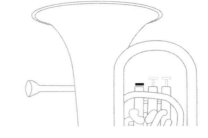

Building Blocks

Use **G** and **F** to play these blocks - slowly at first, then a little faster:

Try these Building Blocks with a metronome or with track 4

Echo Games

With your teacher, buzz, clap, sing or play:

Make up your own Echo Games too

Another Way

Thinking Time

create Echo Games • move between G and F

Learning a new piece

CLAP - Decide a speed for the pulse, count a few bars, then clap the rhythm of the piece to the pulse.

SING - Sing the tune to the note names.

THINK - "Think" the piece, that means "finger" the valves, but don't blow your instrument yet.

PLAY - Count the pulse, take a breath, then play.

Play the first four bars of Another Way (page 12) from memory

Summer Song

Clap, sing, think, then play.

Did the piece sound the way you imagined it? If not, what were the differences?

Moving On

Now play *Moving On* again, this time using any of the rhythms in the grid in any order.

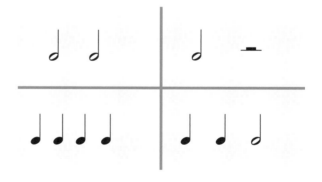

Here on my Own

There are two versions of *Here on my Own* on the CD. What are the differences? Which do you prefer? Clap, sing, think, then play.

The sign above this note is called a *pause*. It tells you to hold the note for a little longer than usual.

Playing A

Have you warmed up properly? Go to page 8

To play the note **A** press down the first and second valves. You will need to firm your embouchure slightly and provide faster air than for playing **G**.

This is what **A** looks like written down:

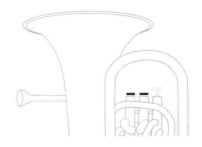

1
2

Building Blocks

Using **F**, **G** and **A** play these blocks slowly, then a little faster.

Try these Building Blocks with a metronome or with track 4

A
G
F

Echo Games

With your teacher, buzz, clap, sing or play:

Make up your own Echo Games too

Note Grid

Each box represents one bar of 4/4. Decide which rhythms to use from the grid on the right and play with the backing on track 4. The empty boxes are rests.

F		F	G		G	A	F	

In this grid, fill in some of the spaces with notes and leave others empty. Decide which rhythms to use, and play with the backing on track 4. Remember to leave some boxes empty as rests.

Mole Hill

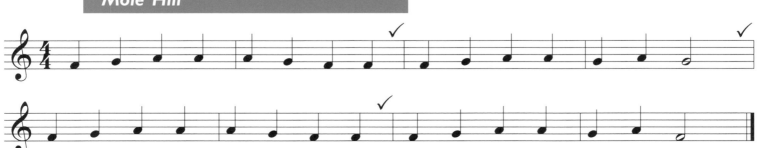

Au clair de la lune

This is a French folk song. Its title means "by the light of the moon".

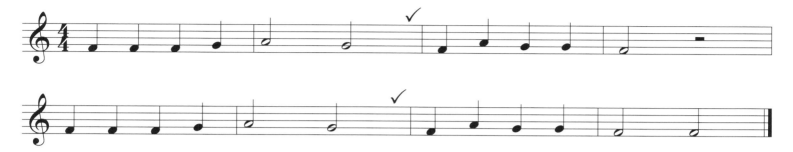

Shore to Sea

Zoom in on the shaded bar. Use the practice hints on the right.

- Play the shaded area slowly.
- "Finger" the valves and imagine how the notes will sound.
- Play them with your eyes closed.

Together

This piece is for you and your teacher. A piece for two players is called a **duet**. Use the practice hints on the right to help you get ready to play it.

- Play your part for the other player, then ask them to play their part for you. Listen carefully!
- Before you start to play, count the pulse together for at least two bars.
- While you are playing, listen to the other person as well as to yourself!

Play the first four bars of Moving On (page 13) from memory

Questions and Answers

Using **F**, **G** and **A**, make up your own "answers" to these "questions". You could include a pattern of notes or a rhythm that you hear in the question.

- Clap, buzz or play an answer on one note.

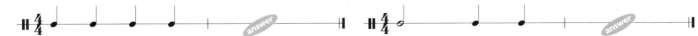

- Play an answer using any notes you know.

Half-beat notes

Half-beat notes are called **quavers** or **eighth notes**. Two or more quavers together are linked together by a line called a **beam**.

A single quaver has a tail.　

Groups of quavers are joined together by beams.　

Feeling the Rhythm

Count a pulse or use track 4 on the CD. Step the rhythms below. During the rests, count silently.

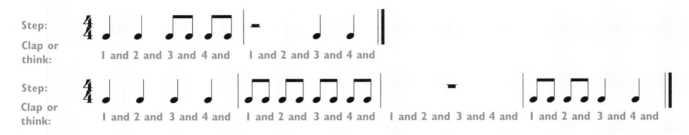

Dolphin Club

Beguine

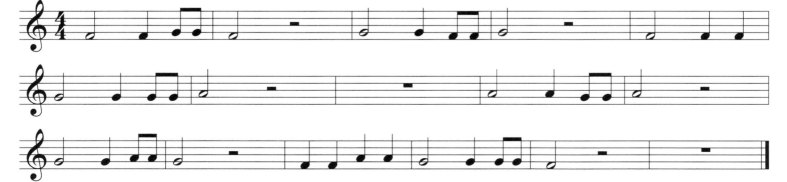

Warm-ups

Buzz two different sounds firstly without your mouthpiece, then with your mouthpiece only:

Higher

Lower

Buzz the following rhythm – slowly, then a little faster:

Always use these exercises to warm up before playing any part of Stage 2

Now play these blocks:

A
G
F

breathe   breathe

Playing E

To play the note **E** press down the first and second valves. To avoid playing **A**, you will need to relax your embouchure slightly and provide slower air.

This is what **E** looks like written down:

1
2

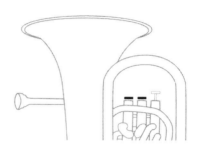

Building Blocks

Using **G**, **F** and **E** play these blocks slowly, then a little faster.

G
F
E

breathe

Try these Building Blocks with a metronome or track 4.

Echo Games

With your teacher, buzz, clap, sing or play:

Make up your own Echo Games too

Down in the Dumps

Chris Morgan

Looking Back

Chris Morgan

Questions and Answers

Using **E**, **F**, **G** and **A** make up your own "answers" to these "questions". You could include a pattern of notes or a rhythm that you hear in the question.

- Clap an answer or play an answer on one note.

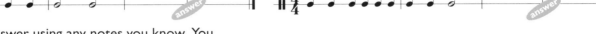

- Play an answer using any notes you know. You could use the starting and finishing notes shown.

Awesome

Zoom in on the shaded notes, using the practice hints on page 15.

Chris Morgan

These two dots are a *repeat sign*. They mean "go back to the start and play the piece again".

Do it Yourself!

Make your own rhythm. Start to clap or buzz some rhythms, trying lots of different ideas. When you find one you like, write it down.

Play the first two bars of *Awesome*. Do the notes move by step, or are there jumps? Now play the first two bars of *Down in the Dumps*. Steps or jumps?

Invent two pieces using your rhythm, and the notes **E**, **F**, **G** and **A**. Start and end on the notes shown. Again, try lots of different ideas.

Start your first piece with notes that move by step:

Start your second piece with a jump:

A new time signature

The 2 at the top of this time signature tells you that there are two beats in each bar.

 2/4 The 4 underneath tells you that the beats are crotchets or quarter notes.

Feeling the Rhythm

Set up a regular 2/4 pulse, by counting "1, 2, 1, 2" out loud. Then clap or buzz the rhythm.

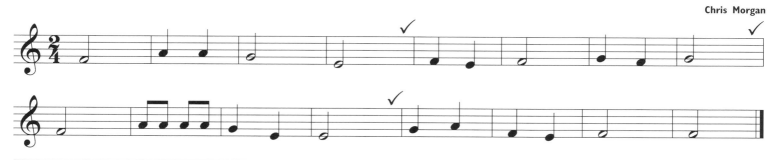

Play the rhythm above, using any note. Then make up your own tune using some of the notes you have learned. You could ask a friend to set up a 2/4 pulse with a percussion instrument.

Little March

Chris Morgan

Again and Again

This piece has a repeated pattern of notes. How many times does it appear? Can you play the piece without looking at the music?

Chris Morgan

on this page:

Playing C

To play the note **C** you do not need to use any of the valves, **C** is another open note. However, to play **C** and to avoid playing **G**, ensure your embouchure is relaxed enough. To hear **C** listen to track 22.

This is what **C** looks like written down:

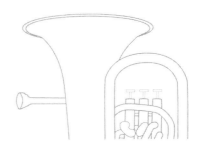

0

Building Blocks

Using **G**, **F**, **E** and **C** play these blocks slowly, then a little faster.

Try these Building Blocks with a metronome or with track 4

Echo Games

With your teacher, buzz, clap, sing or play:

Up and Down

Play the notes below with the backing on track 23.
Count carefully!

Chris Norton

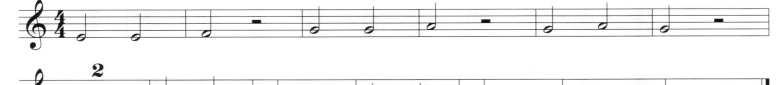

This 2 means there are two whole bars' rest

You can play *Up and Down* using other rhythms too. Try one of the rhythms from the grid in the highlighted bars:

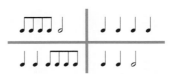

Feeling the Rhythm

Use track 4 of the CD to keep a pulse while you clap this rhythm twice. Turn your palms upwards when you get to the rests.

This sign is a *crotchet rest* or *quarter rest*. It lasts for one beat.

Clap:

Step or think: 1 2 3 4   1 2 3 4   1 2 3 4   1 2 3 4

Step the pulse while you say these words to the rhythm.

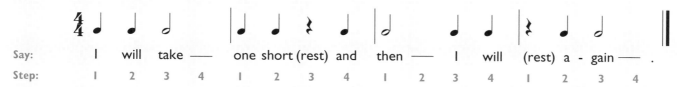

Whisper or "think" the word "rest"

| Say: | I | will | take — | | one | short | (rest) | and | then — | | | I | will | (rest) | a - | gain — | . |
| Step: | 1 | 2 | 3 | 4 | 1 | 2 | 3 | 4 | 1 | 2 | 3 | 4 | 1 | 2 | 3 | 4 |

Beach Hut

You can play *Beach Hut* as a duet, with the CD, or with anyone using a *Boosey Woodwind* or *Boosey Brass* book.

Chris Norton

A new time signature

The 3 at the top of this time signature means that there are three beats in each bar.

$\frac{3}{4}$

Feeling the Rhythm

Do these activities with the pulse on track 25 of the CD.

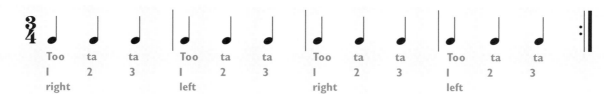

Say:	Too	ta	ta	Too	ta	ta	Too	ta	ta	Too	ta	ta
Think:	1	2	3	1	2	3	1	2	3	1	2	3
Sway:	right			left			right			left		

Fanfare Time

Listen to track 26 on the CD and join in after the fanfare. This time the piece has three beats in a bar.

Listen to the version of *Fanfare Time* on track 26 and then to the version you played in stage 1 (track 1). Can you feel the difference in the rhythm?

Play this four times:

This note is called a *dotted minim* or *dotted half note*. Hold it for 3 beats.

Echo Games

With your teacher, buzz, clap, sing or play:

Note Grid

Each box represents one bar of 3/4. Decide on which rhythms to use from the grid on the right and play with the backing on track 25. The empty boxes are rests.

F	A	G		G	F	E	F

Can you make your own note grid using the rhythms above and any notes you know? Remember to leave some boxes empty as rests.

In and Out

This time, count three beats for each breath.

Breathe in			**Breathe out**			**Breathe in**			**Breathe out**		
count			*count*			*count*			*count*		
1	2	3	1	2	3	1	2	3	1	2	3

City Streets

There are two versions of this piece on the CD. What are the differences? Which do you prefer?

Chris Norton

Icelandic Lullaby

Zoom in on the shaded bar.

traditional

Note Ladders

Choose one rhythm pattern from the rhythm grid and use it to play each note in the note ladders. Move up and down the ladders by step.

Clap your rhythm first, then sing the notes of the ladders. Next, "think" notes and the rhythm. Finally, play your ladders.

Then choose another rhythm. Again, clap, sing, think and play the ladders.

Climb up from here…

...and down again from here.

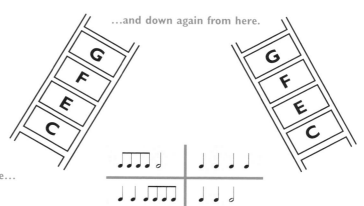

Pacing

Chris Norton

Joining notes together

A curved line joining different notes is called a **slur**. It tells you to move between the notes smoothly.

slur

Smooth Moves

Zoom in on the shaded bar.

Chris Morgan

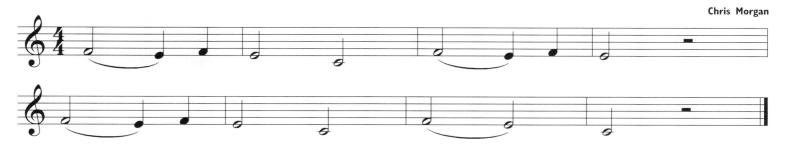

create melodic patterns • play slurs

Warm-ups

Always use these exercises to warm up before playing any part of Stage 3

Buzz two different sounds firstly without your mouthpiece, then with your mouthpiece only:

Buzz the following rhythm - slowly, then a little faster:

Now play these blocks:

Echo Games

Make up your own Echo Games too

With your teacher, buzz, clap, sing or play:

High Jumps

Play these quite slowly.
• Tongue each note.
• When you have played them, start at the end and play the notes in reverse order.

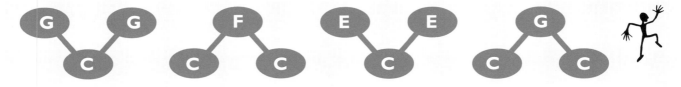

Lazy Days

Zoom in on the shaded bar.

Ian Green

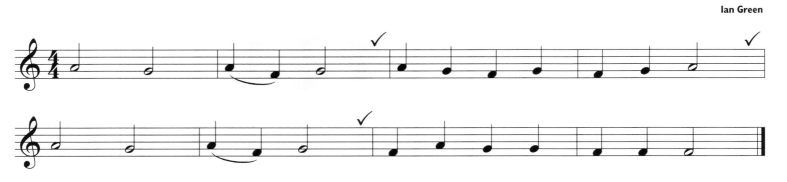

Forest Walk

Ian Green

Four-beat notes

A four-beat note is called a **semibreve** or **whole note**.

A four-beat note has a notehead but no stem.

Sad Times

Zoom in on the shaded bars.

Chris Morgan

Note Grid

Each box represents one bar of 2/4. Decide on which rhythms to use from the grid on the right and play with the backing on track 33. The empty boxes are rests.

E	C	F		F	G		C

Can you make your own note grid using the rhythms above and any notes you know? Remember to leave some boxes empty as rests.

Still Waiting

Zoom in on the shaded bars.

Chris Morgan

In and Out

Practise the following exercise before playing *Calm Sea*.

Breathe in		Breathe out					
count		count					
1	2	3	1	2	3	1	2

Calm Sea

Watch out for the upbeat or anacrusis (say "ana-croo-sis").
There are two versions of this piece on the CD.
    What are the differences? Which do you prefer?

Chris Morgan

Questions and Answers

Using **C**, **E**, **F**, **G** and **A** make up your own "answers" to these "questions". You could include a pattern of notes or a rhythm that you hear in the question.

- Clap or buzz an answer or play an answer on one note.

- Play an answer using any notes you know. You could use the starting and finishing notes shown.

Bicycle Ride

Ian Green

Note Grid

Each box represents one bar of 3/4. Decide on which rhythms to use from the grid on the right and play to the backing on track 25. The empty boxes are rests.

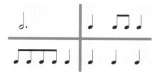

F	A	G		G	E		F

Can you make your own note grid using the rhythms on the right and any notes you know? Remember to leave some boxes empty as rests.

Try recording your melodies

Call to Attention

Watch out for the repeat in this piece. When you come to the ː‖ sign, go back to ‖ː to repeat

Chris Morgan

Do it Yourself!

Find the tunes you wrote in the *Do it Yourself!* activity on page 18, and play them again a few times. Write them down again, but using **C, E, F, G** and **A** instead.

Play and sing the new versions of your tunes. They will sound quite different.

Miles to Go

You can play *Miles to Go* as a duet, with the CD or with anyone using a *Boosey Woodwind* or *Boosey Brass* book.

Chris Norton

Play the Rhythm Grid with a drum pattern on a keyboard

4/4 Rhythm Grid

Buzz, clap, sing or play up, down or across the grid using the backing on track 4. When you sing or play, use the notes **C**, **E**, **F**, **G** and **A**. Don't use more than two notes for any one box.

Try recording your melodies

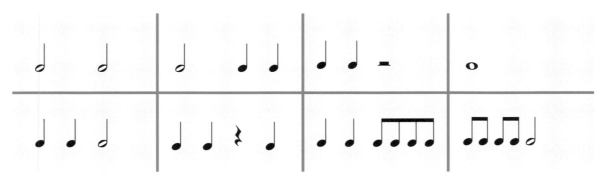

Warm-ups

Buzz two different sounds firstly without your mouthpiece, then with your mouthpiece only:

Always use these exercises to warm up before playing any part of Stage 4

Buzz the following rhythm slowly, then a little faster:

Now play these *High Jumps* quite slowly.
• Tongue each note.
• When you have played them forwards, start at the end and play the notes in reverse order.

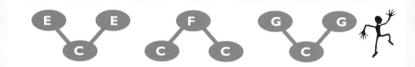

Playing D

To play the note **D** press down the first and third valves. If your instrument has a fourth valve, **D** can also be played using the fourth valve only. Your embouchure will need to be very slightly firmer than for playing **C**.

This is what **D** looks like written down.

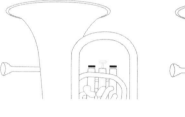

4th valve only

Playing D on the 4th valve can also improve the tuning

Building Blocks

Using **G**, **F**, **E** and **D** play these blocks slowly, then a little faster.

Try these Building Blocks with a metronome or with track 4

Echo Games

With your teacher, buzz, clap, sing or play:

Make up your own Echo Games too

Cactus Tree

Chris Norton

Woogie Boogie

Boogie is a jazz dance style which is often played on the piano. Play *Woogie Boogie* with the drum pattern on the right or with a drum pattern on an electronic keyboard. Experiment with the different styles to see which works best.

Play this 9 times:

high drum

low drum

Anthony Marks

Questions and Answers

Using **C**, **D**, **E**, **F**, **G** and **A**, make up your own "answers" to these "questions". You could include a pattern of notes or a rhythm that you hear in the question.

• Clap an answer or play an answer on one note.

answer

answer

• Play an answer using any notes you know. You could use the starting and finishing notes shown.

answer

answer

Now the Day is Over

traditional

experiment with different styles • move between notes with ease

Bird Food

You can play *Bird Food* as a duet, with the CD, or with anyone using a *Boosey Woodwind* or *Boosey Brass* book.

Chris Norton

Mattachins

Mattachins is a sword dance. Learn to play both parts of the duet.

Optional percussion part (play 10 times):

traditional French

perform in an ensemble

Playing low B

To play **low B** press down the second valve. You will
need to relax your embouchure as if playing **C**.

This is what **low B** looks like written down:

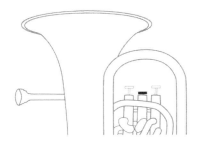

Building Blocks

Using **E**, **D**, **C** and **low B** play these blocks slowly,
then a little faster.

*Try these
Building Blocks
with a
metronome or
with track 4*

E
D   breathe
C
low **B**

Echo Games

With your teacher, buzz, clap, sing or play:

*Make up your
own Echo
Games too*

La Morisque

Tielman Susato

44

Orangutan Rag

Chris Morgan

45

FINE

D.C. al Fine

Go back to the beginning and
play until you reach FINE

Lightly Row

Zoom in on the shaded bars. When you can play this piece, learn to play it from memory by using these practice hints:

- Find any repeated sections.
- Sing the tune in your head.
- Play short sections without looking at the music.

Then play the whole tune from memory.

traditional German

Fast and slow

The speed of a piece is called its **tempo**. Many pieces have words at the beginning to tell you how quickly to play them. These are called **tempo markings**.

Sometimes the words can describe the style or mood of a piece.

Choose a piece you have already learned and play it twice, at two different speeds. Each time, count the pulse before you start so that you feel the new tempo before you play.

Which tempo do you prefer?

Feeling the Rhythm

- Count a pulse of 4/4 and say the words below.
- Say the words while doing the actions.

- "Think" the words while doing the actions.
- Do the actions faster, then slower. How fast or slow can you get and still keep the rhythm?

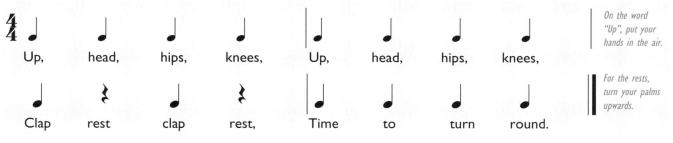

On the word "Up", put your hands in the air.

For the rests, turn your palms upwards.

You could also practise Feeling the Rhythm with track 4 as an accompaniment

Centre Stage

There are two versions of this piece on the CD. What are the differences? Which do you prefer?

Confidently!

Carol Barratt

on this page:

Playing F sharp (F♯)

To play **F♯** press down the second valve. Your embouchure and air support should be the same as for playing **G**.

This is what **F♯** looks like written down.

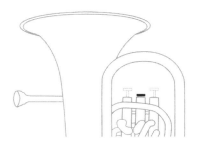

More about sharps

Another name for F is F natural

Play or sing **G**, **F** and **F♯** a few times in any order. Which is the highest note and which is the lowest? Can you hear how **F♯** comes in between **F** and **G**?

♯ When there is a sharp sign in front of F, play F♯.

Building Blocks

Using **D**, **E**, **F♯**, **G** and **A** play these blocks slowly, then a little faster.

Try these Building Blocks with a metronome or with a rhythmic backing track

Echo Games

With your teacher, buzz, clap, sing or play:

Make up your own Echo Games too

Rags 'n' Bones

49

Watch out for the sharp signs in this piece. Whenever you see **F♯**, any following **F**s in the same bar without signs are also **F♯**s.

 This symbol is a natural sign. It tells you to play the natural version of the note.

With precision

John York

part 1

part 2

4/4 Rhythm Grid

Look at the rhythms in the grid. You can work across, up or down the grid in any order you like. Using the backing on track 4 as an accompaniment, try the following:

- Buzz or clap the rhythms.
- Sing the rhythms on any note you like.
- "Think" the rhythms in your head.
- Play the rhythms using F♯.

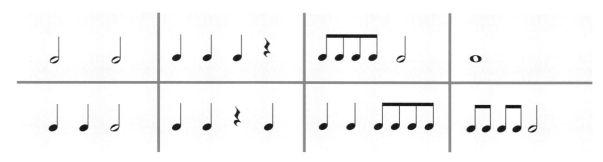

Can you make up a new tune and learn it from memory?

In and Out

Breathe in		Breathe out				Breathe in		Breathe out			
count		*count*				*count*		*count*			
I	2	I	2	3	4	I	2	I	2	3	4

Spooky Route

Carol Barratt

When the Saints Go Marching in

Can you work out how to play this tune starting on
C not **D**?

Cheerfully

traditional

Russian Dance

Watch out for the **F♯**s and remember, any following
Fs in the same bar without signs are also **F♯**s.

With vigour

Dmitri Kabalevsky,
arr. Carol Barratt

Knights Templar March

Proudly

Carol Barratt

Make up your own march using any notes you know
and any rhythms from the grid on the right.

Lip slurs

A slur is when you join two notes together without tonguing the second note. Passing between two notes which use the same fingering without tonguing the second is known as a **lip slur**.

Using your mouthpiece only, pass between a lower buzz and a higher buzz without tonguing. Try to imitate a siren. You could use this exercise as part of your daily warm-up.

Try whistling a low note then a high note. Do you notice what happens to your embouchure?

Higher

Lower

breathe

High Jumps

Play these quite slowly on your instrument.
*   Firstly, tongue both notes of each group.
*   Then, tongue the first note of each group only.
When you slur down your lower jaw drops downwards and outwards. This is called a **pivot**.

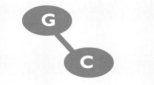  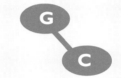 

Practise lip slurs between any other notes you know which use the same valves

Freewheelin'

Try the zoom bars tongued at first, then add the lip slurs.

Simply   Chris Norton

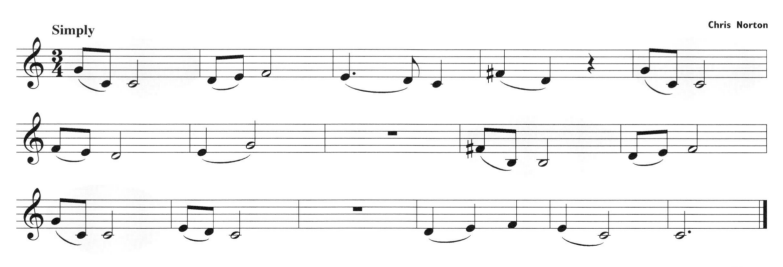

Performance Zone

*   Choose some pieces or activities that you could perform for your family or your class. Choose some solos and some pieces to play with others.
*   Organise a time and place.
*   What will you need? A keyboard, percussion instruments, a CD player, a music stand?
*   Can you tell your audience about the pieces you are going to play? You may need to practise this.
*   Could someone record the performance?

What went well in your performance? Will you do things differently the next time you perform?

Warm-ups

Buzz the following exercise without and with your mouthpiece:

Buzz the following rhythm slowly, then a little faster:

Now play the following *High Jumps*, tonguing the first note of each group:

Playing B

The note B uses the same fingering and slide position as low B

To play **B** press down the second valve. To avoid playing **low B** or **F♯**, ensure that your embouchure is firm enough and the air support is fast enough.

This is what **B** looks like written down:

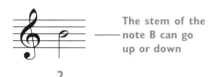

The stem of the note B can go up or down

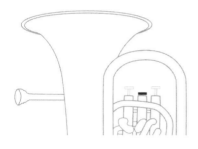

Building Blocks

Using **G**, **A** and **B**, play these blocks slowly, then a little faster.

Echo Games

With your teacher, buzz, clap, sing or play:

Little Brown Jug

Quickly

traditional

Note Ladders

Choose one rhythm pattern from the grid and use it to play each note in the note ladders. Move up and down the ladders by step.

Clap your rhythm first, then sing the notes of the ladders. Next, "think" notes and the rhythm. Finally, play your ladders.

Then choose another rhythm. Again, clap, sing, think then play.

...and down again from here.

Climb up from here...

Land of the Silver Birch

Clap, sing, think then play. You can play this piece as a round.

A **round** is a piece that can be played by several players, starting at different times. This round is in four parts. The numbers show you when to begin.

Steady speed

traditional Canadian

Feeling the Rhythm

A one-beat note with a dot after it (a **dotted crotchet**) lasts one and a half beats. Clap or buzz this rhythm, using track 4 of the CD as a pulse.

Clap:

Say or step: I and 2 and 3 and 4 and   I and 2 and 3 and 4 and   I and 2 and 3 and 4 and   I and 2 and 3 and 4 and

While Shepherds Watched

traditional

Playing B♭

To play **B♭** press down the first valve. Your embouchure and air support should be the same as for playing **B**.

This is what **B♭** looks like written down:

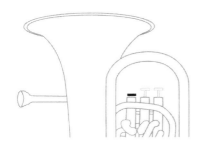

More about flats

Another name for B is B natural

Play or sing **B**, **A** and **B♭** a few times in any order. Which is the highest note and which is the lowest? Can you hear how **B♭** comes in between **A** and **B**?

♭ When a flat sign is in front of B, play B♭.

Building Blocks

Using **G**, **A** and **B♭**, play these blocks slowly, then a little faster.

Try these Building Blocks with a metronome or with a rhythmic backing track

Echo Games

With your teacher, buzz, clap, sing or play:

Make up your own Echo Games too

Yankee Doodle

Sharps or flats at the beginning of a line of music are called the *key signature*. This one tells you to play B♭ every time you see the note B.

traditional American

Quickly

Questions and Answers

- Buzz, clap or play an answer on one note.

- Play an answer using any notes you know.

Aura Lee

Learn to play this piece from memory using the practice hints on page 33. Remember the key signature.

Andante means "at a walking pace".

traditional

Tall Tale, Big Hat

Listen carefully to both versions of *Tall Tale, Big Hat* on the CD. What are the differences? Which do you prefer?

Chris Norton

Imaginary Dancer

- Play this piece slowly, keeping to a pulse.
- Then add in the pauses. What length of pause works best for the mood of the piece?
- Then try changes of speed. Decide how much to speed up and how much to slow down.

accel. is short for the Italian word *accelerando*, which means "speed up".

rall. is short for the Italian word *rallentando*, which means "slow down".

Chris Morgan

remember to play F♯ every time you see F

 Play this piece to someone else and see if they feel that your playing helps them to imagine the dancer.

Playing low B♭

Can you play all the notes you know that use the first valve?

To play **low B♭** press down the first valve. You will need to relax your embouchure and provide plenty of slow air.

This is what **low B♭** looks like written down.

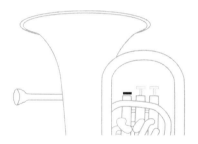

Building Blocks

Using **C**, **low B** and **low B♭**, play these blocks slowly, then a little faster.

Try these Building Blocks with a metronome or with a rhythmic backing track

Echo Games

 *Make up your own Echo Games too*

With your teacher, buzz, clap, sing or play:

Lopsided

Zoom in on the shaded bar.

Anthony Marks

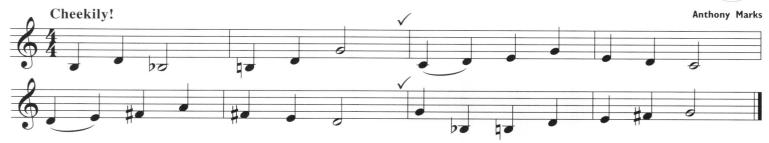

Hopak

Try the zoom bars tongued at first, then add the lip slur from **C** to **G**.

Carol Barratt

A new time signature

The 5 at the top of this time signature means that there are 5 beats in each bar.

$\frac{5}{4}$

Feeling the Rhythm

The rhythm below is in 5/4. Clap the first beat of each bar - this will help you feel it as a strong beat. Then add the sounds.

In this rhythm, the words and actions divide each bar into a group of three beats followed by a group of two beats.

Say:	Dah	ta	ta	Dah	ta	Dah	ta	ta	Dah	ta	Dah	ta	ta	Dah	ta	Dah	ta	ta	Dah —
Think:	1	2	3	4	5	1	2	3	4	5	1	2	3	4	5	1	2	3	4 5
Clap:	clap					clap					clap					clap			

Fanfare Time

Listen to track 64 on the CD and join in after the fanfare. What is the difference between this version and the versions on tracks 1 and 26?
Listen to the other versions again. Can you feel the difference in the rhythms?

Play this four times:

In and Out

Breathe in					Breathe out					Breathe in					Breathe out				
count					*count*					*count*					*count*				
1	2	3	4	5	1	2	3	4	5	1	2	3	4	5	1	2	3	4	5

65 Upstairs, Downstairs

Play this piece with the slurs, then with each note tongued. Which version do you prefer?

Anthony Marks

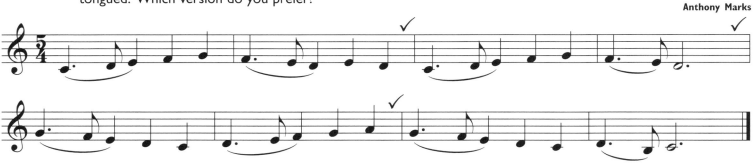

66 Tied up Tight

A curved line joining notes of the same pitch is called a **tie**. Just like a slur, it tells you to join the second note to the first without tonguing it.

Clap, sing, think, then play:

Anthony Marks

67 Fortune Cookies

Moderately

Carol Barratt

part 1

part 2

rit. is short for the Italian word *ritenuto* which means slow down.

a tempo — Go back to the original speed.

The Brass Rap

Lively

Anthony Marks

You can add the following part to your piece. Repeat it as many times as you like. A repeated pattern of notes or rhythms is called an **ostinato**.

You can make *The Brass Rap* into a longer piece if you add the words on the right. You will need to decide how to say them in rhythm. You could also invent a drum part.

How long will your piece be?

Repeating Patterns

How many ostinatos can you hear in the recording of *The Brass Rap* on track 68?

1. Invent your own rhythm pattern to go with *The Brass Rap*. Try lots of different ideas. When you find one you like, write it down.

I hear a tune playing, I hear music,
Beats in my feet and the rhythm's begun!
Taking my time to talk in rhyme,
I've got words on the tip of my tongue.

2. Use your rhythmic pattern as an ostinato.

3. Use your ostinato as an introduction and an ending. When you are happy with your arrangement, make a recording of it.

A new version of a tune is called an arrangement

Loud and quiet

Most music is loud in some parts and quiet in others. In written music, there are special signs called **dynamics** that tell you how loud or quiet it should be. Play these blocks using **G**, then using **C**.

 p This sign means "piano", the Italian word for "quietly".

To play quietly, use *slower air*, but make sure the note is supported.

 f This sign means "forte", the Italian word for "loudly".

To play loudly, use *faster air*, but make sure you keep your tone steady.

 Play some pieces from earlier in the book loudly, then quietly. Which dynamic suits which piece?

Serenade

69

The breath marks in brackets mean they are optional.

Carol Barratt

Leisurely

Tip-toe

Watch out for the changing time signatures in this piece - count carefully! Zoom in on the shaded bar.

Steady

Paul Jones

Warm-ups

Buzz the following exercise without then with your mouthpiece:

Higher

Lower   breathe

Buzz the following rhythm slowly, then a little faster:

Now play the following *High Jumps* *p* tonguing each note. Then play them *f* slurring each pair:

Always use these exercises to warm up before playing any part of Stage 6

Playing upper C

Upper C is another open note. To avoid playing **G** or **C**, you will need to ensure your embouchure is firm enough and that your air support is even faster.

This is what **upper C** looks like written down.

0

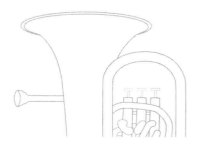

Remember the position of your embouchure and tongue when you whistled a high note (page 37)? This will help

Building Blocks

Using **C**, **G** and **upper C**, play these blocks slowly, then a little faster.

upper C

G

C

Now play them using **A**, **B** and **upper C**.

Try these Building Blocks with a metronome or with a rhythmic backing track

High Jumps

Play these quite slowly.
- Tongue each note.
- Slur each group.

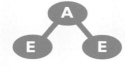
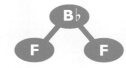
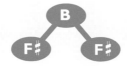

Echo Games

With your teacher, buzz, clap, sing or play:

Make up your own Echo Games too

Scales

A group of notes that moves by step is called a **scale**. Scales can start and end on any note.

How many groups of notes that move upwards by step can you find in *Upstairs, Downstairs* on page 44?

Ski Slopes

- Take the ski-jump up on the left. Create a bumpy take-off by tonguing each note
- Then, imagine that your landing and run down is smooth by slurring the notes on the right.

This is known as the scale of C major

Floral Dance

There are two versions of *Floral Dance* on the CD. What are the differences? Which do you prefer?

Play this p first time through then f on the repeat.

traditional Cornish

When you know this piece, learn to play it from memory using the practice hints on page 33.

A new time signature

In 6/8, the quavers are in two groups of three, so you count two main beats of dotted crotchets.

$\frac{6}{8}$

The 8 at the bottom of this time signature means that the beats are quavers or eighth notes. The 6 tells you that there are six of them in each bar.

Feeling the Rhythm

Clap, say and step the following rhythms:

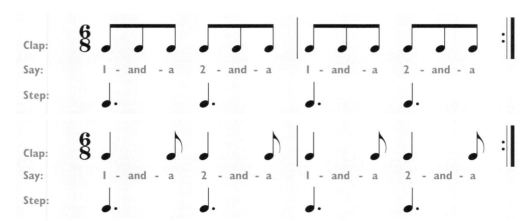

Fanfare Time

Listen to track 72 on the CD and join in after the fanfare.

Play this
four times:

Blaydon Races

traditional English

In and Out

Breathe in						Breathe out					
count						count					
1	2	3	4	5	6	1	2	3	4	5	6

Wave Machine

Play this piece using the rhythm on the right too.
mf (*mezzo forte*) tells you to play quite loudly.

etc.

Anthony Marks

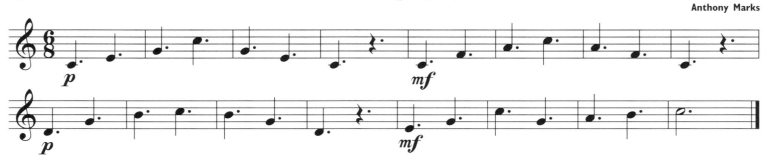

Changing dynamics

Play each *Go-karts* piece as a solo. Then play both together as a duet, starting and finishing each note at the same time.

or *crescendo (cresc.)* means "get louder"

or *diminuendo (dim.)* means "get quieter"

Go-karts, lap one

E
C

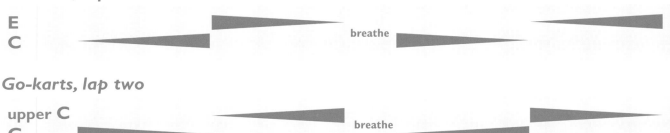

breathe

Go-karts, lap two

upper C
G

breathe

Questions and Answers

Can you work out how to play a song you have learned at school?

Buzz or clap an answer, or play an answer on one note.

Play an answer using any notes you know.

Level Headed

You can play *Level Headed* as a duet, with the CD or with anyone using a *Boosey Woodwind* or *Boosey Brass* book.

Chris Norton

part 1

part 2

High Jumps

Play these slowly, breathing where necessary:
- Tongue each note.
- Slur all notes.
- Start at the end and play the notes in reverse order.

Can you get to the end without taking a breath?

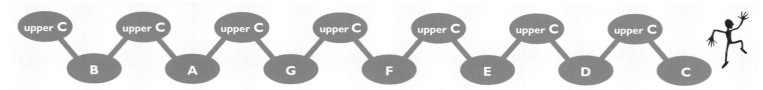

Shaker Melody

traditional American

Thinking about practising

- Could you play this piece differently - a bit faster or slower, for example? Which speed works best?
- Are you making a clear difference between the loud sections of the piece and the quiet sections?

- Are you making a clear difference between the tongued notes and the slurred notes?
- Record your piece and listen to it. Does it sound as you expected? Will you make any changes next time you play it?

Prelude from Te Deum

Play the dynamics in brackets when you repeat this piece.

Marc-Antoine Charpentier

Hine ma tov

Zoom in on the shaded notes.

Allan E. Naplan

Lively, with bounce

FINE

D.S. al Fine

Go back to the sign (𝄋) and
play until you reach FINE

Cool Time

You can arrange *Cool Time* for as many players and
singers as you like. All the parts fit together.

Set a pulse with the drum pattern.

Drum pattern

Chris Morgan

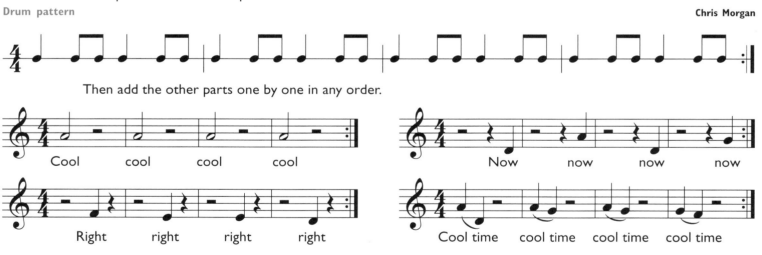

Then add the other parts one by one in any order.

Cool   cool   cool   cool

Now   now   now   now

Right   right   right   right

Cool time   cool time   cool time   cool time

Keyboard part

The keyboard part is on track 79 of the CD.

How long will your piece be? Will all the players and
singers finish together or in turn?

Write some instructions so that everyone knows
when to start and stop. Make a recording too.

Warm-ups

Buzz the following exercise without then with your mouthpiece.
Tongue each block separately,
then slur them.

Always use these exercises to warm up before playing any part of Stage 7

Buzz the following rhythm slowly, then a little faster:

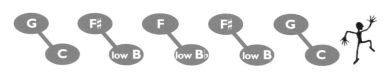

Now play the following *High Jumps* **p**,
tonguing each note. Then play them **f**,
slurring each pair:

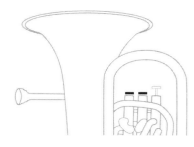

Playing low A

To play **low A** press down the first and second
valves. You will also need to relax your embouchure
and provide plenty of slow air. Remember to pivot
your lower jaw down and forward.

This is what **low A** looks like written down.

Building Blocks

Play these blocks slowly, then a little faster.

Try these Building Blocks with a metronome or with a rhythmic backing track

Echo Games

With your teacher, buzz, clap, sing or play:

Make up your own Echo Games too

Blue 4 U

There are two versions of *Blue 4 U* on the CD. What
are the differences? Which do you prefer?

You could also play this with a drum pattern on an
electronic keyboard. Which style setting works best?

Andante   Anthony Marks

L'homme armé

A round is explained on page 39

This is an old French tune. The title means "The armed man". It can be played as a round. Try it in two parts, with the second person joining in after two bars, then after four bars, and so on. Try it with three parts, or four. Which version works best?

traditional French

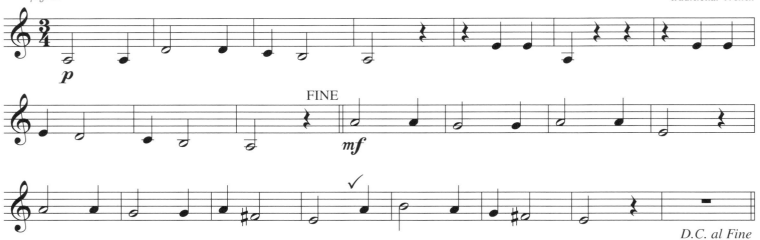

You could also make your own arrangement of *L'homme armé* using **drones**. Drones are long held notes and can be used in different ways:

• Make a rhythm for the drone or add percussion.
• Change the dynamics - perhaps suddenly.

When you are happy with your arrangement, make a recording of it

Mayim! Mayim!

Zoom in on the shaded notes.

traditional Jewish

Questions and Answers

Buzz or clap an answer or play an answer on one note.

Can you work out how to play the theme tune from a soap opera?

Play an answer using any notes.

play with fluency and expression • create musical answers

Kalinka

This is a Russian folk song. When you know this piece, play it without the CD a bit faster. How fast can you play and still keep the rhythm steady?

Experiment with pauses of different lengths. Which length works best?

traditional Russian

A Groovy Kind of Love

Toni Wine & Carole Bayer Sager

first time bar - play this bar then repeat

second time bar - miss out the bar marked "1", go straight to "2"

Penguins on Toast

A dot above or below a note tells you to cut it short, leaving a tiny gap before the next note. This is called **staccato**.

Charming

You can play *Charming* as a duet, with the CD or with anyone using a *Boosey Woodwind* or *Boosey Brass* book.

 This sign is a *quaver rest* or *eighth note rest*. It lasts for half of one crotchet beat.

Chris Norton

Warm-ups

Buzz the following exercise without then with your mouthpiece. Tongue each block separately, then slur them.

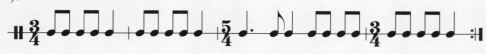

Buzz the following rhythm slowly, then a little faster.

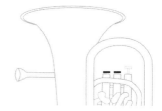

Now play the following *High Jumps* **p**, tonguing each note. Then play them **f**, slurring each group.

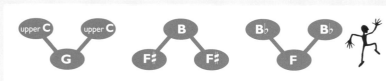

Always use these exercises to warm up before playing any part of Stage 8

Playing upper C♯ and upper D

To play **upper C♯** press down the first and second valves. **Upper D** uses the first valve only. To play both notes your embouchure and air support should be similar to playing **upper C** but you will need to ensure your embouchure is firm enough and that the air support is fast enough.

upper C♯   **upper D**

Can you think of any other notes which use the same valves and also move by semitone?

Building Blocks

Play these blocks slowly, then a little faster.

upper D
upper C♯
B
A

Try these Building Blocks with a metronome or with a rhythmic backing track

Echo Games

With your teacher, buzz, clap, sing or play these *Echo Games*.

Make up your own Echo Games too

In and Out

Take a deep breath in, then breathe out slowly.

Breathe in	Breathe out				Breathe in	Breathe out			
count	count				count	count			
1 2	1 2 3 4 1 2 3 4				1 2	1 2 3 4 1 2 3 4			

High Jumps

Using your mouthpiece only, make a siren sound. How high and low can you go?

Try these High Jumps:
- **f** tongued
- **p** slurred

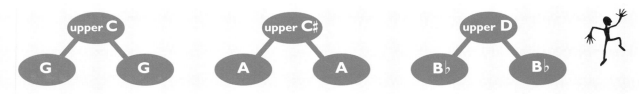

Prince of Denmark's March

Zoom in on the shaded notes.

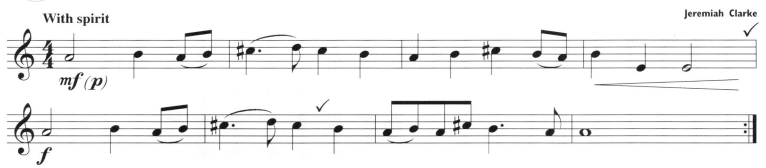

With spirit

Jeremiah Clarke

Hélas madame

There are two versions of *Hélas madame* on the CD. What are the differences? Which do you prefer?

This piece is a duet. If you are playing on your own, play the top part.

Optional drum pattern:

attrib. Henry VIII, arr. Carol Barratt

Bouncy

Cantilena

This tune is taken from *Adiemus* by Karl Jenkins.
Cantilena means "a little song".

Karl Jenkins

Feeling the Rhythm

Some notes begin and end "in between" the beats.
Rhythms containing notes like this are called
syncopations. Clap the rhythms below.

Dodi li

Dodi li is a love song from the Old Testament. *D.S. al Coda* tells you to go back to the sign (%), then when you reach the coda sign (⊕) go straight to the coda.

Nira Chen

Playing, Practising, Performing

Play *Dodi li* in different ways:
- Play it slower, then faster.
- Play with different dynamics.
- Use different lengths of slurs.

Choose pieces from earlier in the book and try them in different ways. When you make new versions of pieces, which do you prefer?

I Love my Love

traditional Cornish

Athol Highlander's Jig

Cheerfully

traditional Scottish

Swing Low, Sweet Chariot

This tune is a spiritual. Spirituals are Christian songs which were originally sung by slaves.

Calmly

traditional

Image

John York &
Anthony Marks

Can you work out how to play your favourite TV theme tune?

Do it Yourself!

Image was written to sound like a television theme tune. What sort of programme could it introduce? What would it work best for, and why? If you made it faster or slower, or louder or quieter, would it still work as well?

Invent your own short jingle or theme for a TV or radio show.

- What kind of programme it is for? Is it serious? Funny? Dramatic? Frightening?
- How will you capture its mood?
- Is it a solo or for more than one instrument?

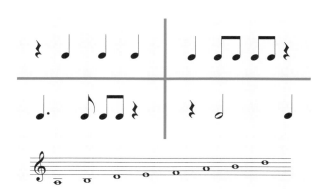

You could use the notes and rhythms in the grid, or any others that you know.

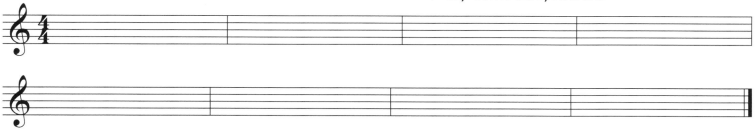

Tragic Consequences

You can play *Tragic Consequences* as a duet, with the CD or with anyone using a *Boosey Woodwind* or *Boosey Brass* book.

Chris Norton

Performance Zone

Put on a show! Here are some tips:

- Decide where you would like to perform and contact the person in charge. Arrange a time for the performance.
- Design some posters to advertise your concert. Where will you put them? Will you need to make some tickets? Arrange for someone to record the performance too.

- Choose what to play. Use anything from this book, or any other pieces you know. Include your own arrangements or compositions, too. If you want to perform duets and trios, have you got enough musicians for the concert?
- Decide what you are going tell the audience about the music. And practise taking a bow!

Fanfare Time

Finally, here is the tune from the first piece in this book.

Chris Norton

CHECKLISTS

Below are checklists for each stage of this book. As you work through each stage, it may help you to put a tick by each activity as you do it. Make sure you have completed most of the activities in one stage before you move on to the next. When you have completed all the stages, you are ready for Book 2!

Stage 1 - ✔ when you have:

- ○ practised *Warm-ups*
- ○ practised *Feeling the Rhythm* with the actions
- ○ listened to some music and counted groups of beats
- ○ practised *In and Out*
- ○ played *Building Blocks* using G and F
- ○ played some *Echo Games*
- ○ used the practice hints (clap, sing, think, play) to play *Summer Song*
- ○ practised the shaded bar in *Shore to Sea*
- ○ played a duet
- ○ made some *Questions and Answers*
- ○ learned at least six pieces

Stage 2 - ✔ when you have:

- ○ practised *Warm-ups*
- ○ played some *Echo Games*
- ○ made some *Questions and Answers*
- ○ practised the shaded bar in *Awesome*
- ○ invented your own piece using E, F, G and A
- ○ practised *Feeling the Rhythm*
- ○ made up your own *Note Grid*
- ○ practised *In and Out*
- ○ played *Note Ladders* using different rhythms
- ○ learned at least six pieces

Stage 3 - ✔ when you have:

- ○ practised *Warm-ups*
- ○ played some *Echo Games*
- ○ practised the shaded bar in *Lazy Days*
- ○ made up your own *Note Grid*
- ○ practised *In and Out*
- ○ compared two versions of *Calm Sea*
- ○ made some *Questions and Answers*
- ○ played a *Rhythm Grid* using C, E, F, G and A
- ○ learned at least six pieces

Stage 4 - ✔ when you have:

- ○ practised *Warm-ups*
- ○ played some *Echo Games*
- ○ made some *Questions and Answers*
- ○ played *Lightly Row* from memory
- ○ played a piece at two different speeds
- ○ compared two versions of *Centre Stage*
- ○ practised *In and Out*
- ○ made up a march
- ○ completed *Performance Zone*
- ○ learned at least six pieces

Stage 5 - ✔ when you have:

- ○ practised *Warm-ups*
- ○ played some *Echo Games*
- ○ played *Land of the Silver Birch* as a round
- ○ practised *Feeling the Rhythm*
- ○ made some *Quesions and Answers*
- ○ compared two versions of *Tall Tale, Big Hat*
- ○ played *Fanfare Time*
- ○ made your own version of *The Brass Rap*
- ○ practised the shaded bars of *Lopsided* and *Tip-toe*
- ○ played pieces from earlier stages using different dynamics
- ○ learned at least six pieces

Stage 6 - ✔ when you have:

- ○ practised *Warm-ups*
- ○ played *High Jumps*
- ○ practised *Feeling the Rhythm*
- ○ played *Fanfare Time*
- ○ played *Wave Machine* with different rhythms
- ○ tried different ways of practising *Shaker Melody*
- ○ practised the shaded bars of *Hine ma tov*
- ○ made an arrangement of *Cool Time*
- ○ learned at least six pieces

Stage 7 - ✔ when you have:

- ○ practised *Warm-ups*
- ○ played some *Echo Games*
- ○ compared the two versions of *Blue 4 U*
- ○ played *L'homme armé* as a round
- ○ made an arrangement of *L'homme armé*
- ○ practised the shaded bars in *Mayim! Mayim!*
- ○ made some *Questions and Answers*
- ○ observed the dynamics and phrasing in *Groovy Kind of Love*
- ○ learned at least six pieces

Stage 8 - ✔ when you have:

- ○ practised *Warm-ups*
- ○ played *Building Blocks*
- ○ practised *In and Out*
- ○ played both parts of *Hélas madame*
- ○ practised the shaded bars of *Prince of Denmark's March*
- ○ practised syncopation in *Feeling the Rhythm*
- ○ played *Dodi li* in different ways
- ○ played *I Love My Love* as a trio
- ○ invented a theme or jingle for a TV or radio show
- ○ completed *Performance Zone*
- ○ played *Fanfare Time*
- ○ learned at least six pieces